Sleight of Hand

Natasha Deen

orca soundings

ORCA BOOK PUBLISHERS

Library and Archives Canada Cataloguing in Publication

Deen, Natasha, author
Sleight of hand / Natasha Deen.
(Orca soundings)

Issued in print and electronic formats.
ISBN 978-1-4598-1120-1 (pbk.).—ISBN 978-1-4598-1121-8 (pdf).—
ISBN 978-1-4598-1122-5 (epub)

I. Title. II. Series: Orca soundings
PS8607.E444S54 2015   jC813'.6   C2015-902478-1
                                      C2015-902479-X

First published in the United States, 2015
Library of Congress Control Number: 2015935533

Summary: Javvan is on probation and struggling to stay out of trouble.
Finding a job is even harder.

*Orca Book Publishers is dedicated to preserving the environment and has
printed this book on Forest Stewardship Council® certified paper.*

Orca Book Publishers gratefully acknowledges the support for its publishing
programs provided by the following agencies: the Government of Canada through
the Canada Book Fund and the Canada Council for the Arts,
and the Province of British Columbia through the BC Arts Council
and the Book Publishing Tax Credit.

Cover image by Getty Images

ORCA BOOK PUBLISHERS
www.orcabook.com

Printed and bound in Canada.

18 17 16 15 • 4 3 2 1

For my family.

Chapter One

I see my chances for a new life die in the eyes of the interviewer. It's always in their eyes. They go flat, lifeless. And it always happens toward the end of the interview. Doesn't matter that I have work experience or that I'm willing to do any job and put in long hours. Doesn't matter that I'm a good student and on the track team. They ask that fateful question, and I have to answer honestly.

That's when their eyes go dead. It's all, "Thank you, Mr. Malhotra. We'll call you."

They never do.

This interview's no different. Bike-courier job. After-school hours, weekend gigs. I could work around my mom's schedule, make sure there's always someone to take my little brother, Sammy, to his after-school stuff. I'd told all of this to the interviewer. She'd smiled, called me a good son.

Not always, but I don't tell her that.

Then she'd laughed, said the job was mine.

Just as I am breathing the tightness out of my chest, she says, "Oh, shoot. Last question." She rolls her eyes, as though it is an annoyance to have to ask me. "Have you ever been arrested for theft?"

"Yes."

The smile holds—she thinks I'm joking. When I don't say, "Gotcha," realization kicks in.

End of smiles. End of her thinking I'm a good son.

"What were you arrested for?"

"I stole a car."

"And you were convicted."

"Yes." I want to tell her more, but it's complicated to explain. Plus, it would make me look like I'm trying too hard to minimize what I've done.

She gives me a look like I just farted. "Thank you, Mr. Malhotra. We'll call you."

"No. Please. I made a mistake," I told her. "Got caught up with a dumb moment—" Stupid. Now I just look like I'm trivializing my choices. "It was a bad decision, and I regret it."

She's standing, ready to shove me out the door. Glancing around like my presence is dirtying her white furniture, white walls, white suit.

"Please. Mrs. O'Toole. Give me a chance." I stay seated, unwilling to budge. This is my twenty-second interview. My twenty-second rejection. If I could go back in time and *not* steal that stupid Lexus, I would. One idiot moment. One stupid choice, and my life's been screwed ever since.

Mrs. O'Toole sighs. Takes off her red glasses and rubs her eyes. "It's not me," she says. "It's our clients. There are sensitive documents that get shipped. We can't take the risk."

"But I didn't steal any files—it was a car—"

"Javvan."

I stop. Use of my first name means it's a for-sure no.

"I have a ton of kids who want this job." She gives me a pointed look. "A ton of kids who didn't steal and didn't get convicted."

Two more years, and my youth record gets wiped. It may as well be twenty years. This thing will never stop following me.

"I have another interview." Her expression is full of pity. "I'm sorry. Good luck—I'm sure someone else will hire you."

"Yeah," I mumble as I stand and head for the door. "That's what the last guy said."

If I could be a coward and wait until my record's expunged before looking for work, I would. But gainful employment is part of my probation. Interviews suck. The disappointed looks of my never-to-be-bosses suck. And what I have to do next sucks more.

It takes about an hour to bike the Calgary streets to my probation officer's building, chain up, then head in. I sit in the room. It's empty except for some cop in uniform. We wait in the dingy outer office with its 1970s decor and 1990s *Reader's Digest* magazines. Fifteen minutes later, my probation officer comes out. Mary Stevens. In my head, I call her Mary, Mary, Quite Contrary. She doesn't believe bad kids can be good. Doesn't believe that good kids can do bad things and still be good. Her favorite word is *recidivism*. That means "once a criminal, always a criminal."

Mary gives me the usual prissy smile. "Javvan. Good. You're here."

The way she talks makes my eyes twitch. High-pitched. False. The dead-giveaway tone that adults who don't like kids use. "Ms. Stevens," I say.

"Come in, sweetie."

She calls all of us *sweetie* when other adults are around. Ditto with calling us *her kids*. Yeah. Right. If that were really the case, she'd have tossed all of us into foster care.

I stand.

She stops. "And don't forget about your phone."

"Right." Mary has a rule about electronic devices in her office. I shut off my phone and drop it in the basket. Rumor is, some kid tried to sneak one in, but Mary had some kind of electronic-detection tech and caught him. Then she reported the violation of his probation. He got booted back to the remand center, where he promptly got his butt kicked and landed in the infirmary.

"You have a job yet?" The nice-girl act falls away as soon as the door clicks shut. Mary gestures to a brown folder as she drops her skinny butt onto the wood chair. "It would look good for you to have employment."

By that, she means it would look good for her. The more first offenders that go straight, the better she looks. And the better she looks, the better her chances of getting promoted.

"No, nothing yet."

She purses her lips. The cheap red lipstick cracks. "You can't find anything?"

"I think that's what no means."

If her lips get any tighter, they'll have to crowbar her mouth open. Or feed her through a straw. I try to hide my smile, but she catches it. Figures it's a smirk.

"If this attitude is anything to go by, then I'm not surprised."

"I'm doing the best I can." I am. I've volunteered at the animal shelter, gotten—after a crap load of begging—letters of reference from my teachers.

"I'm on curfew. I do my homework. I'm doing everything I can."

She sighs. "A couple of the interviewers called. Including"—she glances at the notepad— "a Penny O'Toole."

My spirits lift. She was the last interview. "And?"

Mary's shoulders lift and drop. "I gave you a good spiel. We'll see."

I chew on the hope in her words.

The chair creaks as she straightens. "In the meantime, how are your grades?"

"Mostly Bs, a couple of Cs, one D."

"They need to be higher."

"I know." I try to keep the impatience out of my voice but fail.

This time it's her turn to smirk. "Don't give me attitude. I'm not the one who stole a luxury vehicle."

I don't bother to say anything. This is how she starts her usual lecture.

"You were always on the edge, Javvan. Hanging out with pot smokers, truants."

They weren't the problem. I've tried to tell her this, but she never listens. Those guys were just a bunch of board heads. The problem was the same one most guys face. A chick. Tiffany. Who smelled like vanilla and tasted like chocolate. Her older brother, Dwayne, called me a wuss, said I didn't have the balls to break the law. Made a racist comment about my parents being immigrants.

What I'd wanted to do was punch him. But I'm five foot nine. He's six foot three. And he's got forty pounds on me. So when he bet me $200 I wouldn't steal his neighbor's car, I took him up on it. Figured it was date money. I liked the irony of him paying for dinner for his sister and me.

He never said how far I had to drive the car. My plan was to crack the lock, drive it thirty feet and collect the cash and the girl. What I didn't know was that as soon I went toward the car, Dwayne went to the neighbors, who called the cops.

Outside the courtroom, Dwayne had pulled me aside and said white and brown don't mix. Said I should've stayed with my curry-eating kind.

That's when I'd hit him. Hard. And it had felt awesome. Until I saw the look on my parents' face and the officer coming at me with handcuffs.

I hear Mary say, "That's why so many of you reoffend. Why recidivism is such a problem." There are a couple of sentences left in her weekly sermon, so I tune back in. Nod and grunt. Say I understand. Thank her for her time.

She stands. "Keep trying for work. And stay away from that crowd. It's part of your sentence."

I know. Until I'm off probation, I can't talk to any of them. The last few months of school were crap. I'd see my friends, but I wasn't allowed to talk to them. Tiffany was a bright spot, but her folks had taken the family to Italy for the summer. Not Dwayne. Their parents had sent him to some reform camp. But now I had two months with no friends, no girlfriend.

"Your parents put a lot of money into getting you a good lawyer," Mary adds. "Most kids charged with theft over $5,000 get juvie. You didn't. That's because your lawyer and the prosecutor think you're worth a second shot. Don't let your mother and father down. Don't let the judge or the lawyers down."

I nod and step out of the office.

A kid with a shaved head, tats covering her arms and part of her face, rises. She shoves her phone into the basket and takes my place.

I notice the cop's still there.

She smiles. "How's your hand?"

I blink. "Huh?"

"Your hand." She points to my left. "Thought you might have broken a couple of your fingers."

I still don't know what she's talking about.

"At the courthouse."

"Oh!" My head tilts forward as I stare at her. "You were there?" Think I would've noticed. She's small and pretty, with light-brown hair pulled into a bun. I glance down, register the wedding ring.

She laughs, and it's a nice sound. Heck, it's a bonus to have someone in law enforcement be nice to me. The judge had frowned. The prosecutor had scowled. Even my lawyer had given me the stinkeye.

"I'm not surprised you don't remember." She winks. "Kind of had your hands full, didn't you?"

"Yeah." I laugh. "I guess I did." Then my brain kicks into gear. I don't remember her face, but her voice is suddenly familiar. "You're the one who pulled me off Dwayne."

She nods. "I'm Andrea."

"You're also the one who made sure I didn't get charged."

The humor goes out of her face as she adds, "I heard what he said to you outside the courtroom." She gives me a once-over. "How are you doing?"

"Good."

"Wanna try again?"

"No, really, I'm good."

"Uh-huh. So life as an ex-con is everything you'd hoped it'd be?"

"I could do without the dancing girls every night, but I'm fine."

"It's the high kicks, isn't it? I've heard they can cause neck strain."

She says it so deadpan, it takes me a couple of seconds to figure out she's joking. This gets her laughing. And the whole thing surprises me. Thought for sure I'd get lectured. "It's definitely the high kicks."

"I read your file," she says.

I hide my frown, but I'm confused. Why would she read my file?

My thoughts must show on my face. She smiles, says, "In this line of work, you learn fast which kids are here because they've made a mistake and which kids are here because they're making a career." She pauses. "You made a mistake, and I want to make sure you don't make another one." The smile stays on her face, but her voice takes a hard note as she adds, "I stuck up for you in the court building that day. I want to make sure I didn't make a mistake."

"You didn't—I won't be back here again, not once my probation's up."

She nods, satisfied. "I'm glad they didn't give you jail time. Glad the judge understood the circumstances that led up to the theft."

I shift my weight, rock it to my heels and wait for her to continue.

Her brown eyes flick to Mary's closed door. "She treating you okay?"

That gets my spidey sense tingling. She's not my arresting officer, and she didn't let Dwayne press charges. So why is she checking up on me? No way am I saying anything bad about Mary to anyone connected with the law. "She's fine." In case Andrea's here to test my loyalty, I add, "She's even putting in a good word with some of the people I've interviewed with."

An emotion crosses her face, too fast for me to name it. I think I said the wrong thing. "Uh…" I jerk my thumb at the exit. "I should go."

"Sure—just a second." She digs into her blue uniform and pulls out her business card. "Here. In case."

I take it, shove it into my back pocket and forget about it. Bigger things are on my mind. Being turned down for a job sucks. Mary's disapproval sucks. But going home and facing my parents sucks the most. What I have to do next sucks the most.

Chapter Two

Sammy lifts his head off the couch arm as soon I step inside. Gives me a nod, then goes back to watching TV. The smell of curry's in the air, and I remember Dwayne's slag. For a second, I'm ashamed of the scent of onions, *jeera* and *dhania*, of garlic and chicken. Then I shake it off, because Sammy's asking how the day went. I give him a shrug, then change the channel to the Weather Network just to tweak him.

He shakes his head good-naturedly and grabs the remote.

Mom comes out of the kitchen, wiping her hands on a dishtowel. "How did it go?"

"Fine. One of the companies phoned Mary. That's good, right?" I fake a happy tone. Try to make eye contact. I don't know what it's like for other Indian families, but my family is all about community. A whole. What one person does reflects on everyone. My mistakes have shamed the entire family. It's why I'm trying so hard to get a job. To prove I'm not a waste or a bad guy. I still don't have a job. I still don't have proof I'm good, which is why it sucks so bad to go home.

She nods, forces a smile. "Come." A life growing up in Mumbai lingers in her voice. Like Sammy and me, she's worked hard not to sound too Indian, to be as Canadian as possible. "Dinner's almost ready."

"I thought I'd eat in my—"

"Set the table," she says, then heads back to the stove.

My shoes hit the back of the closet with a *thunk* as I kick them off. I notice Dad in the recliner. He doesn't look up. I don't acknowledge him.

When he'd picked me up at the station, he'd started screaming as soon as we got in the car. He said I'd shamed the family. What was the point of them immigrating to Canada if I was going to be a hooligan? That this mistake would follow me forever.

His voice had gotten more and more quiet as we drove, and by the time we were home, he'd gone submarine silent. He hasn't talked to me since. If nothing else, I want a job to get away from the forced smiles of my mother and the icy quiet of my father.

I follow Mom into the kitchen and set the table. Try not to remember when dinner was full of laughter and arguments. Sammy walks up, helps put the forks and knives in place. "Did you get a job?"

I shake my head.

He peers at Mom, sees she's not paying attention. "Good. If you work, we can't hang out."

That makes me feel a little better. Sammy's almost thirteen, which should make him the annoying little brother. But when we moved from India to Canada, neither one of us spoke English. He was the only one I could talk to, hang with. It's made us more than brothers. We're friends too.

It's been six years, but that outsider feeling's never left me. Not like Sammy. He fits in anywhere. I'm trying to learn how to be easygoing like him. But as my record proves, my emotions tend to get the better of me.

"I learned a new magic trick," he says. "I'll show you after dinner."

Mom lifts her head, gives us a small smile.

Dad stays silent.

As soon as Mom and Dad are finished, I clean the table, then head to my room.

A few minutes later Sammy comes in. "Ready?"

I eye his sweats. "No cape?"

"Still learning the trick. Once it's perfect, I'll do a dress rehearsal."

Even if he wasn't my brother, I'd still want to be his friend. He wants to be a magician. Doesn't care that the kids at school occasionally make fun of him. Doesn't care that he occasionally messes up the tricks. Sammy has visions of being the next big thing in magic,

and he's not letting anything stop him.
I think about this every time I get turned
down for a job. To just keep going.
But that's easy to say, really hard to do.

"Okay." I sit on the bed. "Give it
to me."

"Behold!"

I stifle a laugh. He starts every trick
this way.

"It looks like an ordinary vase—"

"But it doesn't look like a vase."
I can't resist teasing him. "It's got a lid."

He glares at me. "Behold! It looks
like an ordinary pickle jar, but legend
has it that Ali Baba stole this mystic jar
from the sultan."

"I don't think jars can be mystic."

He glares at me. "Are you doing this
trick?"

"No."

"Then shut up."

I shrug and wait.

"Behold! It looks like an ordinary jar, but legend has it that Ali Baba stole this *magic* jar from the sultan."

I doubt it. The jar is black plastic, and I can see the *Made in China* sticker. But Sammy has a story for every trick. He says half of magic is the tale you weave. I lean back on my pillows and listen to the story about this daring theft by Ali Baba.

"And what made this jar so special?" asks Sammy as he moves from the story to the trick. "So valuable that the sultan would send his guards after the thief? It has the ability to transmute solid matter— to change one thing into another!" He pauses, and I make the obligatory sounds of awe and surprise. It's not all faked either. I love watching his tricks.

"Watch as I turn this silk scarf into an item revered by men everywhere!"

"You're going to turn the silk scarf into a bikini model?"

He breaks character and laughs. "Shut up. I'm performing. Besides, if Mom heard you say that about girls, she'd kill you!"

"Don't tell, okay?"

He pretends to consider this. "What's it worth to you?"

"A visit to the Vanishing Rabbit magic shop. Maybe. If your trick's cool enough."

That knocks him back into character.

I watch as he opens the jar, pulls out the scarf, gives it a good shake. He shows me that the jar is empty. Then he puts the scarf back in and closes the lid. Sammy makes some grand gesture that I'm sure is going to result in a back injury, then lifts the lid to reveal two balls.

"Balls?" I ask. "That's the item revered by men everywhere?" Then I get the joke and laugh. "You better not let Mom hear you say that!" I say.

He grins, and I give him a high five.

Mom yells that Sammy has to empty the dishwasher.

He punches me in the shoulder as he takes off.

"Ow!" I call after him. "Maybe if magician doesn't work out, you can go with bouncer!"

Now that he's gone and I'm alone, I'm pathetically happy to strip off my interview clothes. I'm sick of the black pants, the dress shirt and tie. Doesn't matter what I wear. I carry the tattoo of *screwup* on my forehead. After I pull on my sweats, I ball up the clothes and shove them to the back of my closet.

There's nothing to do but stare at the ceiling. Dad took my computer, TV and smartphone. The cell I have is the kind they give kids and seniors. All is does it make phone calls. I'm only allowed to have it when I'm away from home.

Dad checks my usage and calls when I get home, so there's no fun there. I imagine myself six months ago, before my crush on a girl turned me into a moron. I close my eyes, imagine myself with a job.

Almost a week later, and it's the same story. No job. Black looks from interviewers. At dinner last night, Mom asked Dad if he would go to some of his friends, see if they would hire me. He said nothing, just kept eating his food.

The next morning, I chain my bike outside the government building and head in to face Mary. The office is empty, and she brings me in right away.

"Well?" she asks as she closes the door.

"The same." I crinkle my nose against the heavy scent of her perfume.

"I talked to your mother yesterday."

The muscles in my neck go tight.

"She's worried about you. Your family"—Mary's mouth closes, then opens—"is having a hard time dealing with this."

"Yeah." It hasn't exactly been a party for me either. But no one cares about my regret or shame. I'm the idiot who did the crime. So not only do I do the time, but I get the added bonus of not being allowed to be upset.

"Look." Her mouth twists to the side. "I'm going to do you a favor." The desk drawer squeaks as she opens it and pulls out a business card. "This is the name of a contractor I know, Kevin St. James. He got into some trouble as a kid—knows what it's like to try and reform." As she says this, her expression reveals both respect and contempt. "You can try talking to him. See if he'll give you a job."

I snatch the card from her hand. "I'll get on it right away."

"Don't blow this, Javvan. It might be your last chance."

"I won't. I promise."

"Get out of here."

I bolt from the office and grab my phone. I'm anxious to phone Kevin and get my conviction behind me. As I exit the building, it occurs to me that I never said thanks. I'll owe it to her, along with an apology.

Chapter Three

I'm so scared I could puke. Last night after I got home from my check-in, I phoned Kevin, told him Mary had given me his number. Then I blurted out my life story, emphasizing how bad I felt and how hard I was trying to make amends. He agreed to an interview. Which was good. Now I just have to clinch the job.

Kevin's working on a new subdivision east of town. There are no buses that go there yet, and it's too far to bike. Mom drives me and drops me at the trailer that doubles as an office. She gives me a tight smile that's a combination of hope and restrained worry, and says to phone when I'm ready. I nod and wipe my hands on my pants. Then I'm up the metal stairs, knocking on the thin door and stepping inside. The place is cluttered with papers, a worn couch and chair and a scarred desk.

Kevin's a lean man with close-cropped hair, blue eyes. He's got the look of a guy who spends a lot of time outdoors—weathered skin, lines around his eyes. He looks up as I step in. Smiles and waves me in. "Javvan, right?"

"Yes, sir."

He chuckles. "Buddy, this morning I was knee-deep in sewage. You can keep the *sir* for when you're greeting royalty."

I breathe out. Then I take another breath and suck in the scent of oil and sawdust.

"Sit, Javvan." The chair creaks under Kevin as he shifts in his chair. "Mary phoned. I know most of your story. Got the rest when you and I talked."

Thank God. My mouth's too dry to say anything.

"I don't know if Mary told you, but I got myself into a bit of trouble when I was a kid."

All I can do is nod.

"I had someone willing to help me out, knock the chip off my shoulder." He leans back in his seat. "You and I didn't grow up the same. From what I hear, you've got a good family. One that loves you, is supporting you through this."

I brace for impact, for the usual lecture on how I screwed up everyone with one stupid decision.

"I didn't, but you and me, we're the same. We don't like people telling us what to do, don't like it when people offend our sense of honor." He lifts his left hand, shows me his palm. "Got a knife scar to prove it." Kevin gives me a quick smile. "Hopefully, you'll prove smarter than me. Learn to control that temper before it lands you in hospital."

I nod again.

"I like you, and Mary's given me the rundown on your probation. You've got a curfew—that's fine. I don't keep the crew late. No hanging with your old friends." He points his index finger in my direction. "When you're on the clock, I expect you to work. No texting or pissing around. Got it?"

I nod.

"Good. I like what Mary's said about you. So…you got the job."

I manage to croak, "Thank you, sir."

He chuckles. "Again with the sir."

"Sorry."

"Here." He tosses a stack of pages at me. "Fill this out, bring it back. You'll work for me from Monday to Friday through the summer. We're all about honest work here. So we take big jobs, little jobs, warranty stuff—whatever puts food on the table. You work hard, you don't mess around, and if you're good, we'll keep you long-term. Sound good?"

"Yes." I don't touch the papers. My hands are shaking, and I don't want him to see. But I can't believe it. No more begging for a job. No more seeing that look in the eyes of interviewers when they hear about my criminal record. No more of my mom faking happy. I suck in some air, breathe in more oil and sawdust.

"We do new construction, reno- vations, homes that are still under warranty. It takes us all over the city— you know your way around?"

I nod.

"Got transportation?"

I nod again. If I can't take a bus or train, I'm sure Mom will let me use the car.

"I want you to work under the senior guys. Grab and haul the equipment they need, help with the hammering, that kind of thing." He gives me a hard look. "You do nothing you're not licensed or qualified for, you got it? No electrical, no plumbing."

"Got it."

"Good. Make sure you get the equipment—steel-toed boots, hard hat." He sits up, and his chair springs upright. "Now get out. I have work to do." He says it with a grin, and I smile back.

Finally. Things are working out.

By the end of the week, I'm getting the hang of it. Sort of. At first I'd come home in a world of hurt and sore. But each day it's a little better. There's a bunch of added bonuses to working with Kevin. I'm building muscle, which is awesome. When Tiffany gets back, she's going to love my new look. I got a postcard from her last week. Since her family's touring Europe, there's no way to write back and brag about the job or the money I'm making.

She tells me about the trip and what her family's doing. I can read between the lines. I know she's worried I'll dump her because of her idiot brother. I know her parents worry I think they taught Dwayne to be a moron. It's too bad I can't write them back and let them know the only one I'm pissed at is Dwayne.

Today I'm working on a house that's almost done. It's all minor stuff. Painting. Light fixtures. The guys have the radio on, and I'm letting the latest

Top 40 countdown take me into the rhythm of covering the drywall with the pea-green paint the homeowners chose.

"Hey, Javvan, come here."

I set down the roller and head to the electrician. He's from Poland, and we all call him Alphabet—a good-natured dig at his last name, which is more consonants than vowels. "Yo."

"I'm behind on this job," he says, "and we gotta get the fixtures up."

"You want me to paint faster, then get out of the way?"

"No. I'm going to show you how to hook up one of the lights in the hallway. If you can do the other two and the one in the foyer, it would be a huge help."

"Look, I don't have the training for that—"

"It's super easy. I wouldn't have you do it if it was dangerous."

"Yeah, I trust you, but Kevin said—"

"You see Kevin here?" Alphabet asks. "I won't say anything if you help, you get it?"

The implied threat is there. If I don't help, it'll cost me. And everything hits in a wave. The conditions of my probation. What it means if I lose this job. What happens if I attach the lighting and the place goes up in flames.

"Look," he says, "I'll double-check the wiring once you're done."

"If you're going to do that, you may as well do the whole thing." I turn away and hope I don't get clocked in the head. "When quitting time comes, Kevin's going to want to know why I didn't get my job done. I'm not messing with my timeline for you."

He cusses me out, but I ignore him and go back to work.

The rest of the afternoon passes in a haze of paint fumes and churning stomach acid. When it's time to quit,

I pack up my stuff. I want to avoid Alphabet, but I don't want to be a coward. I look for him, figuring I'll make like nothing happened and then we can head out like usual. I find him under the kitchen sink, fiddling with the pipes. He doesn't see or hear me. And my radar goes off. He's an electrician. Why's he messing with the pipes? Instinct makes me back away and keep my mouth shut. I grab my gear and head outside.

Every Friday, Kevin takes the entire crew out for dinner. I hang with a couple of the guys, waiting for the rest to meet up. Alphabet walks past me and heads to Kevin. They lean into each other, talking low and quickly. Then they both look over at me. Alphabet walks away as Kevin waves me over.

"How was the afternoon?" he asks.

"Fine."

"And the painting." He's watching me. "That went good?"

"Yeah, I'm all done 'cept for some trim in the kitchen."

He's still giving me the look. "That it?"

"Yeah."

A long minute goes by, and then he calls Alphabet over. "Alphabet said he asked for your help and you didn't give it."

"I wasn't sure how long the painting would take," I tell him. "You gave me a job. I wanted to get it done."

Alphabet and Kevin look at each other. Then they look at me.

I stop breathing.

Kevin slaps me on the back. "That was a great answer."

"You did good, kid," says Alphabet. "You stood up to me, but you didn't rat me out."

My head is spinning. "It...it was a test?"

Kevin nods. "Trust but verify. I can't put customers at risk or screw with my business. I had to make sure you were trustworthy, and you did awesome. We can start giving you more responsibility. Who knows, maybe construction will be more than a high-school thing for you."

Relief rushes through me. "Thanks." I follow Kevin and Alphabet to the truck and head to dinner. I'm so happy, I think I could fly to the restaurant. No way anything can get me down.

I'm almost swaggering when I go for my check-in with Mary. She's busy with another kid, so I wait. The main door opens and the cop from last time comes in. She sees me, smiles.

"I can tell you've got some good news," she says as she takes a spot next to me.

It's weird that she cares, and I don't know how to handle it. "Uh, yeah. I guess. Got a job and been working."

"Oh yeah?" She's all big smiles. "Where at?"

So weird. Is she following me? Or following up on me?

She must see the wariness on my face. "Relax, kid," she says. "It's a coincidence I'm here." She nods at Mary's closed door. "There are groups of law-enforcement and social-agency workers that meet on a regular basis. Cops, social workers, probation guys." She leans back in her chair. "Inter-agency cooperation is part group therapy, part making sure we're doing all we can to help those in the system. Today's one of the meetings. It's just down the hallway. One of the guys is retiring, and Mary's taking up a collection. I figured I'd come in, donate, then head out." She smiles. "And I saw you, so I thought I'd check in." Her smile turns to a grin. "And check up on you."

"Oh."

"So, tell me more about the job."

"Um, it's with a construction contractor."

"Oh. Who?"

"Kevin St. James."

The frown that crosses her face is fast, but I catch it.

"That's good. I hear he's got a real heart for kids."

I stay quiet.

"So, things are good? Really?"

She's making my insides squirm, and not in that awesome way a pretty girl can do. "All good." Thankfully, Mary comes out of the office.

She glances at the cop. "Andrea. Great. You're here." A quick look my way. "Just give me a sec, okay, sweetie?"

I nod and ignore the sugar tone.

A few minutes later they come out.

"Okay, Javvan. Your turn."

I tell her about everything— including my run-in with Alphabet.

Figure it's got to be good for some kind of bonus points or honorable mention.

She's actually decent about the whole thing. Congratulates me. "You might actually break the cycle," she says. "No recidivism."

I stand. "I'm not screwing this up."

"Good." And there's a weird hitch in her voice. "Make sure you don't."

Over the next couple of weeks I get more comfortable with the job, and Kevin starts giving me more responsibility. He's letting me use the corporate card to pick up supplies, and the truck to grab lunch. A couple of times, people leave their payments in envelopes at their houses, and Kevin lets me collect them. It's a huge nod to his faith in me, and I appreciate it.

This morning we're taking care of a bunch of houses in the northeast. I do a coffee run for the crew and bring it back to the house. The home is finished, but there is some extra work needed, so Kevin sends Alphabet and me. It's nothing major. Alphabet's got to do some stuff in the master bathroom, and I'm touching up the nail holes in the baseboard. But I'm not thrilled.

Something's up with Alphabet. He's messing with the houses. Not all of them, but a few. I don't know why he's doing it, but I see him doing stuff he's not supposed to. Taking wrenches to the water pipes. Screwing around with the flooring. Part of me wants to tell Kevin. He's been good to me, and I want to be good back. Most of me, though, wants to keep my mouth shut.

I keep my head down and do what Alphabet says. Partway through the morning, I run out of spackle for the walls. The extra tubs are in Alphabet's truck. I head upstairs to ask him for his keys. When I walk into the bath-room, he's in the shower stall, doing something to the drain.

I debate walking away, but I have to get my job done. Besides, how would I explain delaying the job? I decide to back away, then call out. That will give him time to stop whatever he's doing. But as I take a step back, I hit a creaking board.

He jerks upright and spins around to look at me with shocked eyes.

"Hey." I pretend I don't see any of it. "Just need your keys."

"Uh, yeah." He fakes a laugh. "Was just tossing a spider down the drain."

I shrug.

He hands me the keys, and I get the stuff I need. I don't head back upstairs. If he's doing something else up there, I don't want to know. Later, when we're supposed to be calling it quits for lunch, I pretend I don't see him from the corner of my eye. Pretend I don't see him go behind the stove and mess with the outlets. He heads out for his lunch, and I'm happy to sit with the rest of the crew and get a break from him.

A couple of hours after lunch, Kevin texts. He says the homeowners' changes weren't covered by warranty. They've left the payment in the office, on the desk. Can I pick it up? he asks.

I've done this for him a couple of times. Sure, I text back. I head to the office, take in the expensive furniture and professional decor. The desk has an Apple computer, a lamp, some papers neatly stacked to the side, but no check.

I text Kevin to let him know.

A second later, the phone rings. "I'm too old for texting. Check the drawer."

"Uh—"

He laughs. "Keep your pants dry. I phoned them, got permission. Jeff thinks he left it in the drawer."

"You sure?" The times before, I've reached into the mailbox or picked up an envelope on a counter. I feel weird about going into their desk.

"No, I'm lying. Geez. If Jeff left the checkbook in the drawer, then that's where he left it."

I know he's straight on, but I still feel a little weird.

"You know what? Forget it. It's not for me to ask you to do something you're not comfortable with."

There's no judgment or tone in his words. Just understanding. Even respect. It's enough to get me moving. I open it—just enough to peer inside. "There's nothing there." To be sure, I move stuff around. There are some books, bank papers, pens, a couple of family photos. "Nothing."

"Okay." He sighs. "I'll have to talk to him again. I hope this isn't some deadbeat thing. I hate having to hammer clients for payment. Look, finish up with Alphabet and head back." There's a pause. "And Javvan? Thanks, man."

I do as I'm told. The next day, it all comes crashing down on my head.

Chapter Four

"Javvan, you better get in here." Kevin's standing on the top step of the trailer. He waves me inside.

I don't like his tone, like he's about to give me bad news. "Okay." I rush up the steps, but my anxiety is making my legs feel like rubber. "What's going on?"

"Just wait." He closes the door. Leans against it.

I sit.

"You're on the clock," he says. "Phone off?"

I nod.

"You sure?"

I pull it out and show him.

"Good. Remember that house we did yesterday?"

"Yeah."

"The wife phoned. Says they're missing some stuff from the home office."

It's enough to make me almost throw up. "Kevin, I was on the phone with you. Whatever they say is missing—"

"Some money and a watch."

"You know I didn't take it. I don't even remember seeing anything like that."

He watches me for a minute, then smiles. "Yeah, I know you didn't." Kevin walks over, puts his hand on my shoulder. "But the problem is your fingerprints are on the drawer handle, aren't they?"

"Yeah." I twist in my chair so I can see his face, but he's already moving to stand in front of me. "But you can explain that. I mean, I was just doing what you told me to."

He leans against the desk, crosses his arms. "I could."

The way he says it—like he knows something I don't—makes my stomach churn. "Kevin?"

"You've been convicted of theft, and now stuff's gone missing."

"But it wasn't me!" Panic turns my voice thin and high. "You know I wouldn't do that kind of thing. You know I didn't do it!"

He shrugs. "We hung up. You could've done something after we'd finished talking."

My brain is spinning, but I can't make sense of it. "I don't understand."

Then it comes together. Alphabet. He's the one who's stealing. My palms are sweating, and I feel like a rat, but it's either him or me. I'm not screwing up my probation. I blurt out everything to Kevin, finishing with, "I don't want any trouble. But it's Alphabet. Not me."

Kevin shakes his head. "I wish you hadn't said that."

"I'm not lying."

"I know." He takes a breath. "That's what makes this so difficult."

"Makes what so—"

"You walked into our little arrangement, and now I have to figure out what to do with you."

The words are English, but they make no sense. "What?"

His face is still smiling, but it's giving me no comfort.

"You know what the trick is to running a great business?"

I stare at him.

"The problem with construction is that it's a feast-and-famine industry. Some days you're rolling in dough, other days you're stopping at the instant-loan places for a quick infusion of moola." He pushes off the desk. "The trick to making it in this business is creating your own work."

He waits for my reaction. I think about Alphabet—messing with the plumbing, the floors. "You damage the houses, then get hired again to fix the mess you created," I say.

He continues to smile.

"But that doesn't make sense. People would know you're scamming—"

"I'm an excellent contractor. I know how to…fix things just right. So does my crew."

"You set it up so the damage happens later, when they won't connect it with you."

Silence fills the trailer. Then it hits me, and I start laughing.

Three wrinkles form in Kevin's forehead. "You wanna let me in on the punch line?"

"You. This." I stand. "It's another test, right? Like with Alphabet? He was setting me up, wasn't he? Checking to see how honest I am."

He gives me a pitying look.

My smile fades. So does my hope. That's why he was asking about my phone. He wanted to make sure I wasn't recording anything.

"I don't want any trouble," I tell him. "Just let me finish my work—or let me go, but don't tell Mary I stole something when I didn't."

"You're not going to be a team player?"

"Please." I'm desperate now. "I can't screw this up."

"Too late. I hate having to go to your probation officer on this." He pulls out his cell. "Maybe we should see what she has to say about the homeowners' complaint."

"No! Wait! I'm thinking!" But it's too late. He's already dialing Mary.

Chapter Five

Kevin uses the FaceTime app, and Mary's face takes the screen. "Got a problem here," he says. "Javvan."

"Javvan? I was just talking to his mother. She's so pleased with how things are working out. You're sure you're having trouble with him?"

"Yeah."

I brace for it. The smug look on her face. The superior lift of her mouth. My heart's going to crash through my chest. But in the back of my mind, I'm still hoping this will all be a prank.

"Give him the phone," she says.

I take the cell from Kevin with shaking fingers and sit back down. I'm too freaked to say anything.

"Didn't we talk about your parents? About this being your big chance to change? About how great the last few weeks have been for you?"

I nod. A sliver of…defiance? desperation?…creeps into my mind. She's already lecturing me, and she doesn't know what she's talking about. "It's not that. You don't understand."

"I understand he's given you a chance," she says. "An opportunity."

"Look." I don't want to do this in front of Kevin. "Can't I come by after work? Talk then?"

She snorts. "You think if you're not doing as he asks, you're going to have an *after work*?"

I lean in and whisper, "You really don't understand."

"I understand your fingerprints were on the desk drawer."

Her words freeze me.

"I understand he's willing to back up your claim of innocence." She pauses. "If you give him equal support."

She knows. Oh my god. She knows. This makes no sense. He phoned her before talking to me?

"Javvan. You want to do right by your parents. You're trying so hard to make amends and show the courts you're not a bad kid. Why would you screw it up now? Do you have any idea what the judge will say—will do—if I go to him with the theft? And turning on Kevin like that. He's got a great reputation with the justice system.

Everyone respects how hard he tries to give troubled kids a second chance."

She sighs. "You try to break the law and screw up. You try to go straight and screw up."

"But I'm trying to be good, to do right."

"Exactly," she says. "Which is why you should listen to him." There's a pause that holds weight. "And do what he says."

And it all falls into place. She's part of this. That's why she knows about the fingerprints.

"You set me up." The words come out flat. Her giving me Kevin's number. Alphabet asking me to help him with the electrical work—all of it was to make sure I meant what I said about doing right. All of it a trap to make sure I was the perfect mark. God, it's Dwayne all over again.

"Don't flatter yourself," she says. "I tossed you Kevin's way because he'd lost one of his crew." Her smile is almost feral. "Recidivism. Such a terrible thing. He needed a body, and you were one. We knew you wouldn't do anything for us."

Kevin nods.

"I've known Kevin a long time," she continues. "You could say we're partners in a lot of things. Our dedication to youth at risk, our love of good steak dinner, an appreciation of how expensive a good steak dinner can be. We also know who our guys are. You're not one of us, and if you hadn't walked in on Alphabet, you'd never have known about the side business." She pauses. "Businesses. Put him on the second crew."

All I can see is a pinprick of light. Everything else has flashed to black. "Second crew?"

"North Americans have so much stuff," says Kevin. "Sometimes it can be such a burden. We help lift those heavy weights."

I listen to the message between his words. Stealing. They're not just messing with the homes. They're stealing from people as well. But I've never heard about any of this in the news. A scam this complicated would take work, organization.

Mary seems to read my mind because she says, "Lots of my colleagues also feel the same way. Not just the probation officers, but social workers, lawyers, even a couple of judges." She smirks.

I'm glad I'm sitting, because there's no strength in my legs. I get what Mary's saying. It's not just her and Kevin running the ring. The members are all through the justice system. I think about Andrea. Is she in on this?

"Do you understand what I'm saying? Just nod if you do."

Nod if I do. I'm trapped. Keep my mouth shut, let him scam homeowners and help him steal, or she reports that I've failed to comply with the conditions of my probation order. Go to another cop or caseworker and tell them what happened and run the risk that they're working with Kevin and Mary. And I still get reported.

"Kevin," says Mary, "he may need the day to think it through."

He takes the phone from my weak fingers. "Don't worry," he says as he shuts down the call. "She's so impatient. You can take the next week." He smiles. "I've been doing this for a long time. You'll come on board. They all do eventually."

I hate that smile. That smile made me trust him. And why give me the week to think it over? I answer the question as soon as it enters my mind. Because he likes the power. Because he's going to enjoy watching me twist for the next seven days.

"As long as you work for me and stay loyal, you're safe. I'm as loyal as you are, and I'll protect you. And I don't want you to be afraid that someone might start talking to you about the arrangement and put you in a delicate situation. I have eyes and ears everywhere. If anyone tried to jam you up, I'd know."

I catch the threat not so subtly hidden in the declaration of protection. If I try to talk to anyone, he'll know.

"Go on, get to work," he says. "Alphabet will be wondering where you are."

I stand on shaky legs, replaying the last twenty minutes in my head. Trying to figure out how the day went from awesome to awful in a blink.

Chapter Six

The day goes by in a blur. I can't focus, can't concentrate. But at the same time, everything is too slow, like a movie played on mega slow motion. The worst part is having to go for the usual Friday-night dinner. All the guys are laughing and having a good time. I'm trying to keep my food—and my contempt—down. By the time I get home, I'm exhausted.

Mentally. Emotionally. Physically. And I'm terrified. I can't see a way out of this.

I drag myself through the door and give Sammy a halfhearted wave. Mom comes out of the kitchen, wiping her hands on a plaid dishtowel. She gives me a smile, and I can barely return it.

Ever since I got the job, my mother has looked different. Her face is brighter, smoother. It used to be I'd hear her pacing late at night. Lately, there have been no sounds of boards creaking.

My brother, cousins and I always joke that there's one big difference between Indian families and other families. In an Indian family, you can be anything you want to be. Any kind of lawyer. Any kind of doctor. Any kind of accountant. My having a record is screwing up the family dream. My getting a job has shown Mom things will get better, that I'll get through this.

The idea of telling her I'm being screwed by my probation officer and my boss takes my strength. I can't break her heart. I just can't do it. I can't bring more trouble and uncertainty to the family.

"Javvan, you're home! Guess what Sammy did in the kitchen?"

"Gross, dude," I say to my brother. "You're supposed to do that kind of thing in the bathroom."

He rolls his eyes and punches me in the arm.

I rub my bicep. "Okay, okay! What did you do?"

"I helped Mom make you some mango *kulfi*."

My favorite dessert. If I had any desire to tell my mother something, it disappears. I glance over at my dad. For a second I debate going to him. But he's hiding behind the newspaper, ignoring me. Telling him would just confirm I'm nothing but trouble.

I go into the kitchen, swallow the creamy dessert. It may as well be cardboard for all I'm tasting. As soon as I can, I escape to my bedroom. I don't bother changing. I just lie there in the dark.

A couple of minutes later, Sammy comes in. "So, what time are we going tomorrow?"

"Going where?"

"To the Vanishing Rabbit."

I frown. "What are you talking about?"

"The magic shop. You said you'd take me."

"No." I shake my head. "I doubt it. I can't stand you. Why would I want to do anything like spend time with you?"

He rolls his eyes. "Be serious."

"I am. You're old enough to know the truth now. I tried to sell you to the neighbors."

For a second, his eyes light up. "Which ones? Liana's parents?"

I flick his ear. "Rein it in, Casanova. If I'd sold you to them, you and Liana would be brother and sister. You couldn't date her." I lean back. "Naw, I tried to sell you to the Olsens."

"Gross." His face screws up. "They're so weird. I'd rather have Liana as a sister than grow up with them."

"That's kind of what the Olsens said too. The idea of having to live with you—you know that's why they go away every summer, right? They're afraid Mom will ask them to babysit you."

He rolls his eyes. "I think we should get to the magic store early."

"Fine," I fake grumble. "If I say no, you'll just cry and you look horrible when you do."

"I'm your favorite brother," he says. "You like doing these things with me."

"You're my only brother," I shoot back as he heads for the door. "I figure being nice to you will get me the bigger inheritance when Mom and Dad die."

"Hey." He turns. "What did you think of my dessert?"

"Tasted great," I lie. "You make it better than Mom does."

"Don't tell her that. Think it's good enough for a job?"

"A job?"

"A backup for when I'm done being a magician. I thought I'd open a restaurant. I don't have a name for it yet."

I shake my head. "You're so weird."

"Sorry, dude. That would make a terrible restaurant name."

"And to think you'll get half the estate."

"You're just jealous because you wish you could be like me."

He doesn't know the half of it. I'd love to play magician and make my problems disappear.

Sammy studies me for a minute. "You okay? You seem strange. Well, stranger than usual."

"Get out. You're stinking up the room."

He rolls his eyes and leaves.

His visit made me feel better. But in five minutes the anxiety and the worry are back. I wish I could talk to my friends, but instinct says to stay away. Mary's shown her hand. I bet she'll be watching, looking for a reason to report me. How am I going to get out of this?

Chapter Seven

I'm not thrilled when Sammy wakes me up at 8:00 AM, but he does it only to annoy me. What doesn't annoy me is him talking about magic.

Sammy's a talker, and he likes people. When we moved to Canada, he was the first one to get the language. Not me. I've gotten used to the fact that he almost never shuts up. In a weird way, it's comforting. A sign that everything's okay. So when he keeps a running patter of what we'll do at the shop, I'm good with it. Especially since it distracts me from my problem with Kevin.

Mom offers to drive us to the store, but that's just more time with her. More chance for conversations I don't want and having to fake emotions I don't have. I opt for the CTrain and take Sammy to Anderson station. It's almost an hour's ride to the store, and the sound of the train on the rails is white noise. Any silence is broken by Sammy and his plans for what we'll do at the shop.

The Vanishing Rabbit is small, but there's enough stuff packed in the space to keep him busy for the morning. Sammy loves to teach, and I'm happy to listen, *ooh* and *ahh* at the right places and help him decide what to buy. It's all fine until a woman walks in.

It takes me a minute to figure out why I know her. Then I realize. It's the cop. Anna. No. Andrea. The one who seems to live at Mary's office. She's got her hair down, and she's wearing makeup.

Why is she here? Calgary's a big city—over a million people. The odds of us running into each other are small. Less than small. I remember what Kevin said about his crew reaching everywhere. And how I don't know who all the members are. There can only be one conclusion. She's here to intimidate me.

A man enters the store. He's brown like me, and he heads straight for Andrea. She smiles as he touches her arm, then reaches up and kisses him.

Okay, maybe she's not here for me.

Then again…

"You okay?"

I jerk back as Sammy's voice cuts through my confusion. "What?"

"You look sick. You okay?"

"Yeah, I'm fine."

He squints at me. "Sure? You look like that time you had too much mulligatawny soup and spent the night puking in the bathroom."

"I'm fine," I say.

"We can go home."

I hate Mary. I hate Kevin. I hate what they're doing to me. "That won't change how I feel," I tell him. "Truth is, it's you. You make me sick." I lean in and sniff his hair. "You smell like wet cheese."

"That's not what your girlfriend said," he cracks.

I laugh, surprised at the joke. The back-and-forth catches Andrea's attention. I see her gaze alight on me. Then she's heading my way.

"Javvan." She smiles at Sammy, who smiles back. "Hi, I'm Andrea."

"Sammy." He jerks his thumb in my direction. "His babysitter."

Her nose wrinkles. "Tell me he's toilet trained."

Sammy shrugs. "Most of the time."

"Thanks, Mary Poppins." I nudge him in the side to shut him up. Then I turn to Andrea. "What are you doing here?"

"Gift for my niece. She's a big magic fan." Once again she turns to Sammy. "She's about eight and just getting started. Any recommendations?"

His face lights up at her asking him for advice.

"Wait a second," I say. "How do you know we're here for him?"

Sammy rolls his eyes. "Come on, dude. You need brains for magic. Anyone who's met you knows magic is out of your league." He's on the road to impress and adds, "This guy. He needs to study for a blood test."

"Hey!" He's trash-talking me with my own trash. That's the same line I used on him last month.

But he and Andrea are high-fiving each other. And just like that, he's made her part of his team. It counts for something. Sammy's got good BS radar. If she wasn't a good person, he would know.

I want to trust her, to believe she would help me. This whole thing makes me feel like I'm drowning and need help getting out of the water. But whether she's a lifeline or a cement boot, I can't tell. And I can't risk that she's part of Kevin's crew.

I stay apart from them. When Sammy starts showing them something called a Spider Pen, Andrea breaks away and comes to me. "Weird that we're both here," I say. "What are the odds of it?"

"Not really that weird." She picks up a deck of cards, squints at it. "There's only a handful of magic shops in Calgary." She turns her squint to me. "What's weird is your tone in asking the question."

My skin flashes cold. "I don't have tone."

She's all cop now. Stone face, laser gaze. "Yeah, you do. What's going on?"

Stupid. I'm so stupid. With Dwayne. With Kevin. Now her. If she's part of the ring, I'm toast. If she's not, I'm still toast. Andrea's got a look in her eyes like she's not going to let it go. I don't trust my voice, so I just shrug.

Her lips go thin. "You in trouble again?"

The *again* is a bullet that tears into me. And in a heartbeat, I know I can't ask for help. It's the memory of my parents at the police station. Even if I ask Andrea for help, she'll have to bring in other people. There'll be an investigation. I can just imagine the look on my father's face. Another disappointment. I can't even make amends properly. And what about the investigation? My word

against a probation officer's and a business owner's. Who's going to believe me?
I stay quiet.

Chapter Eight

Monday at work, and Kevin is everywhere I go. The worst part is how he
makes it look so natural. Just a boss
checking up on his employee, a mentor
making sure his young employee stays
on the straight and narrow.

I even take a job helping one of the
guys shingle a roof just to get space from
Kevin. Doesn't work. Around lunchtime,

he climbs the ladder and "asks" if I'd like to help him do the lunch run.

What can I say? I toss my stuff in a pile and climb down after him.

We get in the truck, and he talks nonstop. Sports. Celebrities. All unimportant. All to show me he's got so much power he doesn't have to talk about anything that matters.

I wish I could get mad. Rage could be my doorway to actually doing something. But I can't get past the fear. I can't find my righteous indignation. Kevin pulls up to a Greek restaurant, and we join the lineup. He takes off for the washroom, and I hold our place. There's nothing to do, so I scan the restaurant and see Mrs. O'Toole. The bike-courier lady.

It's a long shot, but I wonder if I could talk her into hiring me, giving me a chance. Maybe. I ask the guy behind me to hold my place, then book it over to her.

"Mrs. O'Toole."

She looks up from her gyro. When she sees me, her expression makes me take a step back. I'd expected hesitation or maybe wariness. Irritation for sure—after all, I am interrupting her meal. But none of those emotions are in her eyes.

All I see is contempt.

"Yes?" She spits the question.

I'm confused. Last time I saw her she wasn't impressed with me, but she didn't despise me either. Now it's different. The look on her face is the same one Dwayne the Dick had when he challenged me to steal the car. Like I am nothing. Like I am less than nothing.

She shifts away from me. Pulls her purse closer to her body.

Right. Because having a record suddenly means I'm liable to do all kinds of things. Like rob some woman in the middle of a crowded restaurant.

"What do you want?"

"To tell you I got a job." The words are out of my mouth before I can stop them.

Her upper lip curls for a second. "How wonderful for you."

Her tone implies the opposite.

I'm confused and angry. What's with the attitude? But it seems stupid to pick a fight here. Besides, Kevin will be back soon, and the last thing I need is for him to see me talking with Mrs. O'Toole.

There's nothing else to do, so I turn to walk away. Then I stop and spin back to her. "You're a smart lady, Mrs. O'Toole."

She frowns.

"I'd think you'd know the difference between screwing up and being a screwup. I'm one, not the other." I walk away before she can answer.

I'm back in line when Kevin returns from the washroom. He scowls at the fact that I'm still not at the cashier. "What's taking so long?"

I shrug. Then I have to get away. The room is suddenly smaller, hotter. My stomach's rolling at the smell of onions and lamb. "Be back in a sec."

He grabs my upper arm as I move away. "Where're you going?"

"Bathroom. Geez." I pull out of his grip. "A little late to worry about leaving me unattended, don't you think?"

He has no answer, and I walk away. From the corner of my eye, I see Mrs. O'Toole watching us. There's something about her posture that jacks my interest. I go toward the bathroom, but instead of going in I do a five count, then peer around the corner. Sure enough, she's making her way over to Kevin. The crowd is my cover as I sneak back to them. I hover in the background and eavesdrop.

"—you made the right decision?"

I frown, certain Mrs. O'Toole isn't questioning Kevin's decision to have Greek for lunch.

"These kids need a second chance," says Kevin. "That's what I'm giving him."

"I'm not arguing that," she answers. "But in his case, I think you're making a terrible decision."

"Javvan? No. He's a good kid. Just made a bad choice."

"That's what I thought too, until I talked to his probation officer."

My insides turn to ice.

"She said Javvan's the kind of kid who'll only break his mother's heart. She said it's just a matter of time before he ends up back in the system. That any attempt to rehabilitate him is just a waste."

She said. The words are clanging in my ears, drowning out all the noise of the crowd, the sizzle of meat on the grill.

"I'm not here to tell you how to run your business or who to hire," she says, "but reconsider what you're doing."

"I thought about it, trust me." Kevin's words are smooth, and I hear the smile in his voice. "And believe me, I took Mary's words into account. But I have to believe these kids can change. Javvan's been a good kid. Works hard, shows up on time, pitches in." He steps toward her. "I've lent him the truck to do food and supply runs, gotten him to pick up checks from clients. He's never let me down."

I can almost hear the clang of the jail door slamming shut. It's a beautiful setup. He's painted himself as the good guy. If anything goes wrong, I'm the one who'll come off as deceitful and manipulative, not him. It'll be me who abused his trust, played the mind games. He'll be the regretful adult who tried to give some kid a second chance and got burned.

Mrs. O'Toole shakes her head. "I hope you're right."

Kevin turns sober. "Yeah." he says, "Me too."

And in that moment, I find the thing I've been looking for. My anger.

Chapter Nine

All this time, I'd thought I couldn't get a job because of my record. And for sure, my conviction played a role in it. But Mary hooped me. She bad-mouthed me to potential employers, and why? To get me to work with Kevin.

They need good kids who've made dumb mistakes. Kevin said he wanted my type for the ring because we wouldn't be involved for long. What a load. He wants kids like me because we give him plausible deniability.

If he used some cranked-up kid who was always in trouble with the law, when things went wrong Kevin would look like the idiot. "How could you not have seen it?" people would ask. But—*but*—when he uses a first offender from a relatively good background, he looks like a saint. The kid looks like the sinner.

Kevin and I get to the front of the line, put in our order and collect the food. When we're back in the truck, I ask, "How long have you been doing this?"

"Picking up food for my employees? Since forever."

"No. The other stuff."

He shoots me an amused smile as he eases the truck from the parking spot and onto the road. "What other stuff?"

I figure he's playing coy. Two can play. "Your business."

Another amused smile. "You got your phone on *Record*?"

I shake my head. "You're too smart for that."

The corner of his mouth pulls up. "You're right about that."

"So? How long?"

We're at a red light, and he holds out his hand. "Phone."

I shrug. "I'm not the liar." I hand him the phone. "You are."

He takes the phone, glances down and shuts it off. Then he reaches into the center console, pulls out a small black box and aims it at me. When nothing happens, he says, "Just checking."

"Thought I was wearing a wire?"

"Or a second phone." He shoves the device into the console. The light goes green, and he turns his attention back to the road. "Can't be too careful."

"Told you, I'm not the liar."

"No. You're just the moron who took the bait from a racist and jacked a car."

I hide my anger and say, "Can't argue that. Back to the original question. How long have you been in business?"

"Why do you care?"

I don't—not really. But I don't have a real plan on how to get him. Yet. I figure getting him talking and doing it with no agenda—no recording device, no tricks to get him to confess—will mess with him a little. Maybe it will also downgrade me in his eyes. If he thinks I'm dumber than I look, maybe he'll give me the foothold I need. Anyway, it can't be too bad an idea to get some background. Who knows when it'll come in handy?

"I care because you screwed me over," I say. "And you did it like I was a chump."

"You are a chump. Eager to prove yourself to those around you, eager to please the people in your life. That's why you got into trouble in the first place, right? If you hadn't cared about that numb-nuts, you wouldn't have taken his stupid bait and fallen into his trap." Kevin snorts. "In the grand scheme of things that moron didn't even matter, but you cared, and look where it's gotten you."

The truth hurts, and coming from this guy, it stings.

"You gotta look out for number one," says Kevin. "Or else you'll never be anything but a loser."

I want to point out the irony of his calling me a loser. But it'll put him on alert, remind him I have brains in my head.

"Look." His tone is comforting, and it makes my skin itch. "This isn't forever. You do your stint with me, Mary clears your probation, and you're done."

Bull. No way these clowns let you off once they have their hooks in you. "Wish I could believe that."

"You see any twentysomething-year-old dropouts working for me?"

"No," I say as my brain does the math. If he's talking about guys in their mid-twenties, then he's been doing this for five to ten years. Okay. My mind goes dead on what to do with this information.

If Tiffany were here, she'd know exactly what to do. She loves mysteries and tech crap. She'd get all my friends together and pull off some kind of sting. Except she's not here.

But my friends are.

The tightness in my chest loosens. Right now, Kevin and Mary need me. Which means I've got a little room to wiggle. If I'm smart about it, maybe I can connect with my buddies, get some help on this. I lean back, look out the windshield and start the countdown for the end of the day.

As soon as work's done, I get out of there. I head to Shaw Millennium Park. It's our place to hang during summer. The skate park's crowded. I feel a rush at the sound of wheels on concrete and the cheers and jeers of the boarders. I miss my crew, miss catching air and carving. Miss nailing a trick. Miss feeling normal.

I scan the crowd for my buddies. Smile when I see Wheezer's fauxhawk. Just as I'm heading over, my phone rings. I pull it out, figuring it's Mom. "Yeah?"

"Javvan. Where are you?"

I freeze at the sound of Mary's voice. "What do you want? It's not time for my check-in."

"It's always time for your check-in." She pauses. "Where are you?"

"Downtown."

"Where downtown?"

"West side?"

"You wouldn't happen to be at the skate park, would you?"

My throat's immobile. I can't make a sound. For a mad second I think she's followed me. Then I realize she can probably hear the noise of the park. I find my voice again. "I'm walking by it. Heading to Eau Claire Market."

"That's a half-hour walk," she says. "Why didn't you take the bus directly there?"

"I meant to, but I guess it's force of habit—got off at the wrong stop." I stop myself before I start babbling. Liars always talk too much.

"Watch your habits," she says. "I'd hate to see them lead you down the wrong path."

I flip the phone shut. Consider my options. Right now, there aren't any. It was stupid to answer the phone, but that's what happens when your dad won't spring for caller ID. But his decision has screwed me up. I can't risk asking my buddies for help. Mary's onto me, which means I must have tweaked Kevin's radar in the truck. Doubly stupid.

I catch sight of Wheezer. He's watching me. He lifts his hand in salute. I wave back, then keep walking.

Chapter Ten

I walk in the door and immediately feel the tension. Dad's got the newspaper up, covering his face. Mom's facing the stove. The scene is like always, but this time there's a brittle silence.

"Where's Sammy?" I ask Mom.

"His room." She looks up from the *baingan bharta* she's making and gives me a tired smile.

If Sammy's hiding, the parents have been fighting. "Is it me?" I ask him as I walk into his room. "They're fighting because of me again?"

He looks up from his comic book. "Yeah. Mom wants to sell you to the neighbors, but Dad figures we can get a better price if he takes it international."

"Lame."

"Tell me about it. There's 1.27 billion Indians in India. The market's full of brown."

"Ha-ha." I shove him aside and flop onto the bed. "I meant your snark is lame. I already used the selling-to-the-neighbors line on you a couple of days ago."

"Dang," he says. "I thought it was weak when I said it. Now I know why. It came from you."

"Was it bad? The fight?" I ask.

He shrugs.

Yeah, it was bad. "I'm sorry. What I did was totally stupid, and it's screwing up everything—"

Sammy rolls his eyes. "You, doing something stupid. What a news flash." He punches me on the arm. "Forget it. Okay?"

But I can't. And now the shadow is getting darker. "Got a question for you. How would you—" Then I stop. He's just a kid, and getting him involved in this mess feels wrong.

"Don't leave me hanging. How would I what?"

I sit up. "Never mind. It's stupid."

"So are you, and yet, here we are. What's going on? Is it the job?" He catches my stare of surprise. "You couldn't lie to save your life," he says.

No wonder Kevin saw through my lame ploy.

"What's going on? The boss doing something he shouldn't?"

I stare hard enough at him that I think my eyes are going to pop out of my head.

Sammy sighs. "It's the only thing that makes sense."

"Let's talk hypotheticals."

Now it's his turn to stare at me.

"What?" I say.

"Nothing," he says. "Just surprised you know what *hypothetical* means… you do know what it means, right? You're not just repeating words to seem cool?"

"Loser."

He grins.

"I need to get someone to confess," I say.

"Duh. Use the voice-record feature on your phone."

"But they have equipment that detects stuff like that."

"Oh. Well, that's harder."

"So, genius? What do you have?"

He leans back on the bed, closes his eyes. "What are they doing?"

"I don't want to say."

He opens his eyes. Watches me. "Sucks, bro. I'm sorry."

"You don't have anything to be sorry for. You didn't do anything."

"Still…"

"Thanks."

"So is this what happens when you like a girl? You do dumb things to impress her?"

"You definitely do dumb things to impress girls, but what I did—it had nothing to do with her. I was stupid and macho, and she was totally pissed that I let her brother egg me on."

"And now you're stuck with a bad boss."

"Something like that."

"Can't you just tell your probation officer?"

I shift and say nothing.

"Oh." He closes his eyes again. After a minute, he says, "The boss is doing something bad, and the probation officer doesn't care."

"Yeah."

"And you can't go to the cops—"

"The word of an offender against that of an upstanding citizen, and I have no proof."

"Why not?"

"Huh?"

"Why don't you have proof?"

"He makes other people do the…uh, bad things."

Sammy sits up. "Any way to make it look like he's doing it?"

"Huh?"

"What's he making you do?"

I hesitate.

"Javvan, come on. You're already 98 percent in on this with me. Go all the way."

I tell him everything and finish with, "Now they want me to steal."

"And you have to do it or they say you violated your probation and frame you for theft."

I nod. "Something like that." I think about Mom and Dad, then force myself to stop thinking.

Sammy gives me a smile. "Sometimes you're so dumb, it's cute."

"Wow. Thanks for the love, bro."

"What you need to do is basic magic. Wear gloves—"

"Well, no duh—"

"—and plant his prints all over the stuff. Then report him."

He's got my attention. "What? How do I get his prints on stuff without cutting off his hands?"

"It's super easy to do. Get something he touches. Lift his prints. Stick it on the stuff you're supposed to steal.

Go to the cops." He frowns. "We'll need to figure this out. A good trick is all about the magic."

We. I love that word in a new way.

"We need to visit the magic shop." Sammy hops off the bed. "So? We gonna do this or what?"

I grin and follow him out the door.

Chapter Eleven

When we get home, I spend the next while with Sammy, learning how to steal the glass off the table.

"You have to be quick, smooth and fast—"

"That's how I got Tiffany." I smile.

He snorts. "Please. That classy chick? That was her pitying you. The key to a sleight-of-hand trick is distraction.

Get the guys at the table looking one way while you scoop the glass." He sets a mug on the kitchen table and makes me practice sweeping it into my hoodie with a napkin. "Be careful—don't smudge his prints or get yours on it."

When I get the movement figured out, he ups the level. I have to do it during dinner without Mom or Dad noticing. No surprise that the first time, they both notice. Dad says nothing. Mom frowns and warns me about spilling milk on the floor.

"But if you do," Sammy says, "we won't cry over it."

We all stare at him.

"Get it? Cry over spilled milk?"

I hide my grin behind a mouthful of chocolate cake. Mom and Dad smile.

Since both Mom and Dad caught me, Sammy makes me practice after dinner. Three hours of rehearsals, and I can do it with ease.

Chapter Twelve

Friday's the big day. We head to some chain restaurant that Alphabet swears has the best steak. Kevin orders nachos and potato skins. He orders beer for the adults and sodas for the any one underage. I keep an eye on his glass, ready for the end of the night. My hope is that everyone will be busy—putting on their jackets, paying, downing the last of the food. The contained chaos will give me the cover I need to snake the glass.

I run into the big problem a half hour into the meal. The waitress. She's not just bringing fresh pitchers, she's bringing fresh glasses. Crap. How am I going to get the beer mug now? I take a breath and consider my options. There's only one— get the glass from her. The problem with this is that she's a good waitress. She's got the tight outfit and tighter work ethic to prove it. She takes the glasses from us, heads directly behind the bar and dumps them into the washer. I watch Kevin's glass, and my chances for freedom disappear in a wash of hot water.

"Javvan, man, you with us tonight?" Kevin claps me on the back, all friendly-like, and brings me back to reality.

"Yeah, I'm here."

He scans my face.

"Girl problems," I say.

It's the truth. The watchful look in his eyes dims, and he turns his attention back to Alphabet.

I return to my problem. I can't just ask for the glass. Can't go behind the bar. And I only know the one magic trick Sammy taught me—how to make the glass disappear.

It takes me a couple of minutes, but I figure out the solution. If this works, I'm going to have bragging rights for the next week. I eat the chips, drink the soda and wait.

When she comes with a new pitcher, I wait and let her collect the dirty dishes. I grab two napkins. With the first one, I make like I'm wiping my mouth, then stuff it into the glass Kevin used. Now I'll know which one is his. The second one I stuff into the kangaroo pocket of my hoodie. The waitress turns to leave. I give it a five count, then follow her to the bar. "Hey."

She turns, smiles.

"Can I grab some change?" I pull out a twenty.

"Sure, hon. What do you want?"

I shrug. "Not sure. I guess enough to pay my share"—I give her what I hope is a charming smile—"and the tip."

Either the smile works or she's too much of a pro to roll her eyes. "How about a ten and two fives?"

"Sure, that works."

We exchange the money, I turn, then turn back. "Sorry. You know what? Can I break a five?"

"No prob." As she goes to hand me the change, I pull my hand away. The coins scatter to the floor.

"Crap! Sorry!"

She—ever the pro—bends to collect the coins.

I give a quick glance at the table. No one's watching me. All eyes are on the baseball game on the big screen. I whip out the napkin, swipe the glass and then put it in my kangaroo pocket.

My silent cheer of victory is short-lived when I realize how awkward it is to carry the glass around in my pocket. But luckily for me, the restaurant is darkly lit, my hoodie's black, and no one seems to notice the sudden bulge at my midriff.

When I get home, I immediately head to Sammy's room. I brag about my trouble-shooting, then pull out the glass with a triumphant "Ta-da!"

He just rolls his eyes. "Asking for change. That's something a five-year-old would have thought of in thirty seconds. Trust you to take two minutes." Sammy moves to his closet and pulls out the stuff we'll need.

I figure it will be some tape to lift the prints and a sheet to hold them until they're needed. Of course, I've under-estimated Sammy. He's got a whole setup, including superglue, graphite powder and a camera. It takes us a few hours, and it's time wasted. Maybe on TV it looks easy, but faking fingerprints in real life is almost impossible. At least, it is for us.

Sammy sees the defeat on my face. "Don't worry," he says. "We'll figure out a way."

Maybe. But we only have two more days, and I'm back with Kevin, Mary and this whole terrible thing.

Chapter Thirteen

It takes forever to fall asleep, and just when I do, Sammy starts shoving me, trying to wake me up.

"Go to Andrea," he says when I finally sit up.

"The cop?"

"She's good people—I feel it."

I push aside the covers. "Your feelings don't count. Kevin and Mary said there are other people—justice people—involved. Andrea might be one of them."

"Or she might not be." He sits at the end of the bed. "Besides, she was the one who stepped in between you and Dwayne. She vouched for you when she didn't have to. I'm telling you, she's good people."

"You remember her from the courthouse?"

"Not to put a stake through your heart or anything, bro, but your theft rocked the family. Trust me, I remember everything about that day."

I put my face in my hands. "I'm such a screwup. The first Malhotra in our family to be on the wrong side of the law."

Sammy punches my foot. "Don't whine. You did it, you're making up for it. Don't let some sleazeball boss screw you over. Go to Andrea."

I watch him for a minute. "You got your cell phone?"

"In my room."

"Go get it."

"You're going to call her now?" His eyebrows rise with disbelief. "It's 2:00 AM."

"I'm going to call her station and find out when she's working, and then I'll go in and see her." I hold up my hand. "And then I'll decide if she can be trusted or not."

Sammy goes to get the phone and I dig into the laundry hamper, looking for my pants. I find them crumpled in the bottom, and in the pocket is Andrea's number. I know I shouldn't get too excited, but the idea she could be trusted, that she might believe me… I check the card. It's got the main line and her direct number.

When Sammy comes back, I dial her directly. The phone rings four times, and then the voice mail picks up. My optimism sinks as I listen to her message.

"What happened?" Sammy asks when I hang up.

"She's away for the next few days."

"Oh, right. At the magic shop, she was talking about the gift for her niece. I think they live in Edmonton. I guess we're back to square one, unless you don't mind stealing for Kevin for the next few days."

"Yeah, right." I hand the phone back. "Thanks for trying."

"Yeah," he says glumly. "No problem."

After he leaves, I lie in bed trying to think of a way around Kevin, but all I see is my probation getting revoked and me in juvie. I fall into a fitful sleep.

"If you're going to keep doing this," I tell Sammy when he wakes me a second time, "at least bring some chai."

"When do they meet? Your boss and your probation lady?"

"I don't know."

"Okay, well, the scanning device. Is it just in his truck?"

"I think so."

"And it's not always on?"

I think back. "No, he had to turn it on. Why?"

"Simple. We stick your phone—your old one that Dad has—in his pocket and record him talking to Mary."

"That's not going to work on a bunch of levels. What do I do, walk up and shove it in his pocket?"

"Exactly."

"You're a lunatic."

"It'll work. Just listen to my plan and then tell me if you disagree, okay?"

I nod. What do I have to lose? By the time Sammy's done going over his idea, the hope is back. This might actually work. And if it does, not only can I get out from under Kevin and Mary, but I stand a good chance of bringing them down.

Chapter Fourteen

The next day, I take the car to work. We're in the southwest this time, dealing with a flooded house. Now that I know how Kevin operates, I wonder if he's the one behind the flooding. When Kevin's finished dividing up the tasks, the rest of the crew goes to their jobs, but I hang back.

"I want to talk to you," I tell him.

His mouth lifts into a half smile. "Unless it's to tell me you're on board, I have work to do."

"I want to meet with you and Mary." My hands are sweating, and I hear the tremor in my voice.

This gets me a smirk from him. "Why?"

"I want to make sure my butt's covered in all of this."

"I told you—"

"Yeah, and I'm telling you, I want the meeting."

He steps in. The smile's still on his face, but his eyes are hard.

The sun's bright and behind him, and I have to squint to maintain eye contact.

"Remember who you're talking to, boy. I can get you reported."

"Maybe." I swallow. "But I'm the one who can raise a stink. And sure, it's your word against mine. And yeah, maybe you and Mary have been smart about hiding the evidence, but whispers can destroy a company. When no one wants to hire you 'cause they're not sure if you're a good guy or a bad guy, what's that going to do to your bottom line?"

The smile vanishes. "Fine. In a couple days—"

"Today. After work. I want this over and done with."

He stares me down for what feels like forever. "After work." He bites out the words.

I hold my breath as he turns away, and I don't let it go until he's out of sight.

At the end of the day, Kevin comes up. "Let's go."

"I've got my car."

He shrugs. "Suit yourself."

I follow him to Mary's office and park as far as I can from him while still keeping him in view. Kevin gets out, crosses the lot and starts for the main doors. I give him a few seconds to get ahead of me, then follow. The sidewalk's mostly quiet. A few walkers, some skateboarders.

As he gets closer, one of the skateboarders starts doing tricks. His buddy pulls out a camera and starts filming, and the first part of Sammy's plan goes into effect.

Chapter Fifteen

Sammy's the one with the camera. Wheezer's doing the tricks, and he makes sure to skate and then wipe out. Right into Kevin. They both go down. Sammy and the rest of my friends run to them. They pull Wheezer and Kevin up and make a big show of dusting off my boss, asking him if he's okay.

He's irritated. He mouths off to them a little, then heads inside.

Sammy looks away from Kevin and catches my eye. He nods.

Part two, complete. My phone—wiped of all personal information except a voice-activated recording app—has just been slipped into Kevin's pocket. As soon as Kevin starts talking, the phone will start recording everything he says.

I head inside and to Mary's office. Kevin's standing by her desk. Mary's sitting.

She scowls when she sees me. "Shut the door."

I do.

They watch me.

"Look." I lift my hands. "I just—"

"Where's your phone?"

I jerk my thumb at the outer office. "In the bin. Just like always." I turn out my pockets, lift my shirt and jeans. "I got nothing on me."

They glance at each other.

"I might be dumb enough to steal a car," I say, "but I'm not stupid. You guys have my life and my future in your hands. I'm not doing anything to mess with you."

The answer seems to satisfy them, because their shoulders drop.

I let my hands fall to my side. "Why not just let me finish the work and go? I promise I won't tell."

Mary rolls her eyes. "You know our dirt. The only way to protect ourselves is to share some of the mud. You get on board, or I bury you so deep you won't come up for air until Christmas." She sneers at me. "Or whatever holiday you people celebrate during winter."

"Fine." I ignore the racial slight. "Then all I want are some assurances."

"Like what?" Mary's question comes out like a sneer.

"Like, I don't do anything to mess with the houses. I don't want to break any faucets or pull out drywall or anything. And I'll steal the small items, but the big thefts are on your other crew. I'll scope the places, make notes about the good stuff, but that's it."

Kevin rolls his eyes. "You don't have the experience to do anything to the houses. You think I'm going to let you run amok and burn down a place?"

"I'm just saying—"

"You'll take a few little things, easily missed items," says Mary. "We've been doing this for a long time. You think we're stupid?"

"No." I take a breath. "And I'm out once the probation's up. No calling me back—"

Mary snorts. "Kid thinks he's Michael Corleone." Her gaze snaps my way. "Yes, Javvan. Once you're out, you're out."

And I want out. Of this office. My stress level is high, and I don't think I can take any more. I nod at them. "Okay, that's all I wanted."

Mary rolls her eyes. "Get out."

I book it out of the office, out of the building. I need to stay and make sure the last part of the plan goes off without a hitch, though, and that means moving the car. When Kevin comes out, he can't see that I'm still here. I pull out of my parking spot and wedge myself between a van and a truck. Then I wait. A half hour later, Kevin walks out.

My friends are still there. Sammy runs up, extends his hand. He's apologizing, saying how sorry they are, and, please sir, don't make trouble or complain to the cops. He's got Kevin hooked. They're shaking hands, and after Sammy claps him on the back, he reaches into Kevin's pocket and slips the phone out.

I take a breath and another one.

Once Kevin's gone, I leave too. Head to the spot we agreed on and wait for Sammy and the guys to come.

They pile into the car a few minutes later.

"Here." Sammy hands me my phone. "I made backup copies, just in case."

I pocket the cell, then drive everyone home.

I can't believe we've done it.

Chapter Sixteen

Sammy and I are almost home when his phone rings. He picks it up, says hello, then listens. Then he looks at me and gestures for me to pull over.

"Yeah," he says as I find a safe spot to park. "He's right here. Hold on." He hands me the phone.

I take it. "Hello?"

"Javvan, it's Andrea. Your number—well, your brother's number showed up on my cell. I recognized the last name and thought, given our last conversation, that I should phone. What's going on?"

I glance over at Sammy, then take a breath and tell her everything. When I'm done, she says, "Go home. I'm going to call my partner, Shane Quimpere. He's going to meet you there. Tell him everything, and we'll get this sorted."

"Are you sure he can be trusted? Mary said there's a bunch of law-enforcement guys involved—"

"I'll bet money there isn't anyone but these two yo-yos." Andrea's voice is flat with dislike. "They're messing with you 'cause you're a good kid who made a bad choice and they can manipulate you. Go home. We'll get it sorted."

I hang up and hand the phone back to Sammy. Then I do what she says.

By the time we pull into our driveway, the cop is already there, waiting on the steps with Dad. Sammy heads into the house. I ignore my father and tell Shane I want to talk to him alone. We head to his car and I tell him everything, including them framing me for the stolen items.

He asks me a few questions, listens to the recording, then takes the cell. "We'll figure this out," he says. "I promise."

We shake hands, and then I head back to the house. Dad's still waiting on the steps. I push past him and head inside.

Chapter Seventeen

I don't say anything as I step past him and into the house.

"What just happened there?"

It's the first thing he's said to me in months. I should be mature, but I can't help but give the smart-alecky answer. "An arrest."

Anger flits across his face. "Why was that guy here?"

"Why do you care?"

"Don't be smart—"

"It's an honest question. You haven't given a crap about me in months. Why care now?" The words rush out of my mouth. It feels too good telling him off for me to stop. "One mistake, that's all I made. One—"

"Giant mistake, Javvan! Your future, everything your mother and I worked for—"

"And I didn't work for my future?" I was hoping to stay in the anger, but the hurt of his silence comes through in the cracking of my voice. "I was a good son. I did my best, and I'm sorry that I'm not perfect. And I'm sorry that I made a stupid mistake. I'm sorry I made a big, stupid mistake. But I'm tired of being sorry. I've done everything I can to make it right, and I haven't had any help from anyone but Sammy and Mom. So you know what? Screw your questions and your curiosity." With that, I stomp to my bedroom and slam the door.

He doesn't follow.

Part of me is happy I got the last word. Most of me is sorry that silence seems to be the only thing left between us. I close my eyes and wish the day away.

Mom comes in a couple of hours later, and I tell her everything. She cries when I tell her I didn't think I could trust anyone. She cries harder when I tell her about the fight between Dad and me.

Dinnertime comes, and I go to the silent table. We pass around the dishes of naan and rice, *aloo rasedar* and tandoori chicken. Before I can start eating, my dad says, "I was angry. But I was also scared." He looks at me. "Mostly scared."

Mom and I glance at each other. Sammy eats.

"I…mishandled the situation," Dad continues. "We both made mistakes, and I want you…I'm sorry." He bends his head and turns his attention back to his meal.

It's not a Hollywood reconciliation, but it'll do.

Sammy grins at me over his cup of tea. I grin back and start eating. After a few minutes, Dad asks about what happened this afternoon. I start from the beginning, hesitant at first, then picking up speed as I register that he's not going to start yelling. By the time I get to needing Sammy's help, my brother jumps in and takes over the story. Through it all, my mom says nothing. She eats, and though her head is bent, I see the small smile that curves her lips.

Within a couple of weeks, it's all over the papers. Kevin's in trouble. Mary's in trouble. A few kids have come forward. Plus, I have Andrea on my side. She helps me get a new probation officer, and the interviews for jobs start again. I'd hoped the judge would take pity on me, commute my sentence. Though he acknowledges the role I played in bringing down the bad guys, he says I'm still responsible for the mistake I made. It pisses me off, but deep down I know he's right. Which pisses me off more. And kind of makes me smile.

On the bright side, he's modified my probation so I can see my friends, and Dad's given me back my phone. Tiffany and I have been emailing. So other than the humiliation of having to find another job and sit through all those horrible interviews, I guess it's all good.

I sit at the computer, emailing my résumés. I hope if anyone recognizes my name, they'll focus on the fact that I helped bring down a theft ring and not that I stole a car. The home phone rings, and Mom answers it. She listens, then hands it to me.

I take it from her. "Hello?"

"Javvan?"

I try to place the familiar voice.

"It's Penny O'Toole. You'd applied for the bike-courier job—"

"Yes." I frown. Mom catches my look and frowns back.

"I, uh, read about what happened in the paper."

I don't say anything.

There's a long silence, and then she says, "Javvan, I'm sorry. I'd wanted to hire you, but after your probation officer talked to me—"

"Yeah, I know."

More silence.

"Would you like a job?" She asks the question in a timid voice, like she's waiting for me to get mad. "I don't have the bike courier, but—"

"Yes. I'll take it."

She laughs. "You don't know what it is yet."

"I don't care. The interviews are humiliating. You want me to scrub toilets or take out trash, I'll do it. I want this thing behind me, and I'll do what it takes."

Silence. "Okay." There's understanding in her voice. "You're hired."

"What am I doing?"

"Working as my assistant. Someone told me there's a difference between being a screwup and just screwing up. I figure anyone who knows that difference would work well as my assistant."

I don't know what to say. Instinct tells me this job will pay more and carry me farther than the bike-courier job. "Thanks, Mrs. O'Toole."

"When can you start?"

"I'm spending today with my brother…" I have no idea why I'm telling her this, except maybe so she knows for sure that I'm a good guy. "But I can start tomorrow, if that's okay."

"My office, 8:00 AM sharp." She hangs up.

I make a mental note to get there by 7:45 AM.

Sammy comes up. "Ready to go?"

I feel like things are turning around. Like all this crap is finally going and I can let go, get on with my life. I stand, grab my jacket. "Yeah," I say. "Let's make like a rabbit in a hat and disappear."

He rolls his eyes. "That's so bad, I can't even respond."

I laugh and follow him out the door.

Acknowledgments

With great thanks to my remark-able editor, Andrew Wooldridge, for his insights and my gratitude to Jared Tkachuk for helping me understand the nuances of the restorative justice process.

Award-winning author Natasha Deen graduated from the University of Alberta with a BA in psychology. In addition to her work as a presenter and workshop facilitator with schools, she has written everything from creative nonfiction to YA and adult fiction. She was the inaugural 2013 Regional Writer in Residence for the Metro Edmonton Library Federation. Natasha has lived in South America and the United States and now calls Edmonton, Alberta, home. For more information, visit www.natashadeen.com.